This song is dedicated with love
to each and every one of my pets,
especially my cat Fifi who was my best
friend for nineteen years.

—Buffy Sainte-Marie

BUFFY SAINTE-MARIE

Hey Little Rockabye

A Lullaby for Pet Adoption

illustrations by BEN HODSON

GREYSTONE KIDS

GREYSTONE BOOKS • VANCOUVER/BERKELEY

Hey hey little rockabye,

Hey hey little darling,

Hey hey little rockabye,

You got somebody loves you.

Were you born on a cold winter day?
Are you a poor little orphan?

Did somebody throw you away?

Now you got somebody loves you.

Hey hey little rockabye,
Hey hey little darling,

Hey hey little rockabye,
You got somebody loves you.

When they dropped you off at the shelter,
All you had was your little fur coat,

But now you got somebody loves you.

Hey hey little rockabye,
Hey hey little darling,

Hey hey little rockabye,
You got somebody loves you.

You got somebody loves you.

Author's Note

This is a song that I sing to all my animals when I first welcome them home. I have had lots of pets: dogs, cats, puppies, and kittens from my local shelter; more than thirty goats and their kids; and the most wonderful horse in the world who lived to be forty-six years old. All of them have been rescues who needed a home and they each have filled me with special joy. Some were at the shelter waiting to be adopted. Others needed a home because of other reasons, but I sure have loved each one of them every day, and I've felt very lucky that they have been my pets.

You can sing "Hey Little Rockabye" to a kitten or puppy, or a grown-up cat or dog, or a rabbit, or a guinea pig, or a horse—any kind of pet. My horse was very big but I still sang "Hey Little Rockabye" to her pretty often. I also sang it to each one of my goats. I think there's nothing as cute as a baby goat, and they sure like to cuddle.

You can make this song fit your pet. You might want to sing "Hey hey little rockabye boy" to your boy pet, or "Hey hey little rockabye girl," which is what I used to sing to my girl cat, Fifi.

ANDERSON COOPER

No matter what kind of animal your little rockabye pet is, or whether you have a boy or a girl, and no matter how young or how old, or how big or how small your pet is, I hope my song will make you feel loving and cozy together and fill you both with special joy, too.

ME AND
MY ANIMALS

BLUE

PENUCHE THE LAUGHING CAT

PUA NANI & FIFI

CAPTAIN KID & LOLA

ME & A KOALA AT THE LONE
PINE SANCTUARY IN BRISBANE,
AUSTRALIA. I ONLY GOT TO
HOLD HER FOR A FEW MINUTES.

Hey Little Rockabye

WORDS AND MUSIC:
BUFFY SAINTE-MARIE

Greystone Kids / Greystone Books Ltd.
greystonebooks.com

Cataloguing data available from Library and Archives Canada
ISBN 978-1-77164-482-2 (cloth)
ISBN 978-1-77164-484-6 (epub)

MIX
Paper from
responsible sources
FSC® C012700

Buffy Sainte-Marie is managed by Paquin Entertainment
Proofreading by Antonia Banyard
Jacket and interior design by Sara Gillingham Studio
Jacket illustration by Ben Hodson

Printed and bound in Malaysia on ancient-forest-friendly paper by Tien Wah Press

Greystone Books gratefully acknowledges the Musqueam, Squamish,
and Tsleil-Waututh peoples on whose land our office is located.

Greystone Books thanks the Canada Council for the Arts, the British Columbia Arts Council,
the Province of British Columbia through the Book Publishing Tax Credit,
and the Government of Canada for supporting our publishing activities.

Canadä

Canada Council   Conseil des arts
for the Arts   du Canada

BRITISH COLUMBIA   BRITISH COLUMBIA
                    ARTS COUNCIL
                    An agency of the Province of British Columbia